D1313726

Rahoola's SONG

For my parents
and for my first grade teacher, Mrs. Phillips,
who dubbed a little boy "Artist Anke"

Text and illustrations © 2013 by Robert Anke

Published in the United States by Cupola Press®

www.cupolapress.com

Library of Congress Control Number: 2012911022

ISBN-13: 978-0-9857932-0-3

First Edition   10 9 8 7 6 5 4 3 2 1

Printed in Malaysia

Rahoola's SONG

By Robert Anke

Cupola
PRESS®

LAFAYETTE, CALIFORNIA

In a forest with trees pointing up to the moon,
there lived and there sang an uncommon raccoon.

Listening closely, you could hear him each night,
his voice softly weaving its way through the heights.

High in his perch at the top of a tree,
Rahoola sang simply to set a song free.

But down in the forest, things weren't quite the same.
The moonlight was scattered. The dark played a game.

There, between shadows, shiny things glistened,
and scarcely a raccoon would bother to listen.

In half a moonbeam, the shiny things looked
like treasures for taking. The raccoons were hooked.

They'd snatch the stuff up,
then scuttle about,
searching for more 'til the
search wore them out.

With armloads of shiny things
clutched in their clutches,
they'd carry it home
to put in their hutches.

Their fireplace mantels flaunted the stuff,
and no matter how much,
it just wasn't enough.

After a while, the shiny thing habit
became the raccoons' "Stop-Look-and-Grab-It"

The "Shine-It"

The "Show-It"

The "Need-Me-Some-More"

The "Go-Out-and-Get-Some"

The "Locking-the-Door"

And that's how it went, with time passing by—
shadows below and Rahoola up high.

'Til one night it changed when a visitor came.
She appeared and intoned, "Morticia's my name."

"I've come with sad news. Your cousin was dinner.
Some bears in the woods—trying not to get thinner—
had him with mustard. We found half a bottle.
They filled up on him, then away they all waddled."

"The good news is, you were left in his will
a house full of things on Withering Hill."

All said and done, she faded from sight,
as he watched her through tears
of fractured moonlight.

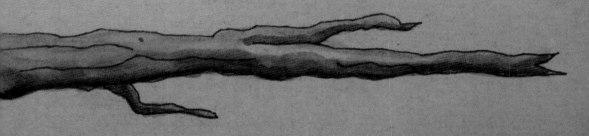

His heart feeling heavy, he sank to the ground.
The song of the forest became just a sound.

What was the purpose if life would just end?
And what did he have to show for *his* then?

Rahoola dragged on, each step a new chore,
then arrived at his cousin's and opened the door…

He stood there in awe, his mouth open wide.
Thousands of shiny things shone from inside!

The shiny things winked,

and with that he forgot

everything he was,

and all he was not.

"I'll find more tonight! I'll search until dawn!"
Rahoola's sweet singing was suddenly gone.

So the ride started, around and around,
the wanting-a-thing until it was found.
Then finding it, peace would return for a bit,
but sure enough, soon, the wanting would hit.

Over and over and over again,
he filled up the bedroom, he filled up the den.
He filled up the kitchen, the bathroom, the hall,
until the whole house had no room at all!

Then one fateful night when he came home with more,
the things inside had spilled out the front door.

Rahoola was exhausted, ready for bed,
so he laid his new shiny things under his head.
He slept in the open, sprawled out on the ground,
and kept on snoring when morning came around.

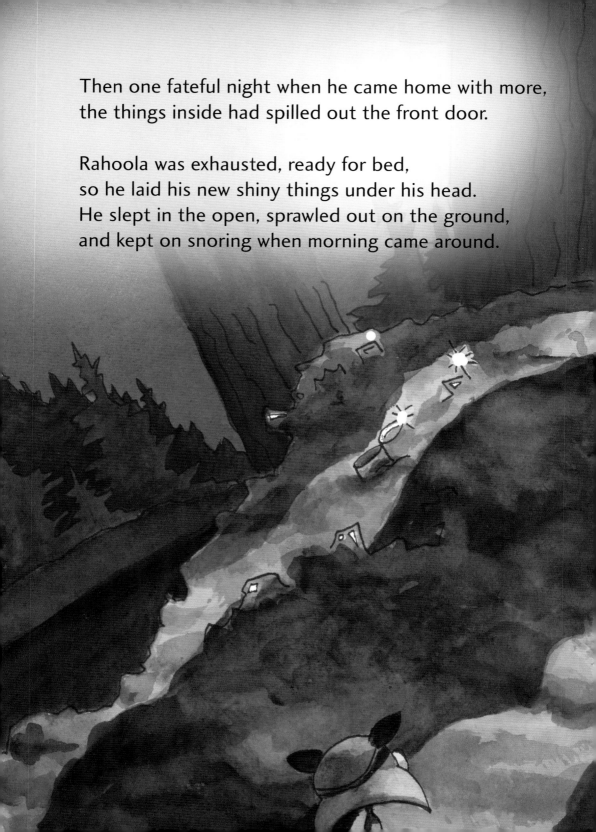

By the time it was noon, with the sun overhead,
Rahoola was dreaming in yellow and red
of hot things like chiles and deserts and thirst
and an egg in a pan that fried 'til it burst.

Then he woke with a jump, crying,
"TURN OUT THAT LIGHT!!!
My goodness it's warm…
Who made it so bright?!"

As he squinted his eyes,
he wondered what stunk.

And what in the world
was this huge pile of…

...JUNK!?

Crinkly plastic and aluminum foil?
Bits of old foam dripping with oil?
A sticky old peach pit all covered in fuzz?
"WHO PUT ALL THIS TRASH
WHERE MY SHINY STUFF WAS?!?"

"Who took them? My treasures!
Where'd they all go?!?"
He scrambled from pile to pile screaming,

"NOOOOOOOOOOO!"

Then he just stopped and stared at the mess,
the untidy, disordered heap of excess.

And he finally got it:

his shiny thing stash

was really just one

giant pile of *trash*.

So he packed it in bags, and he packed it up good,
and took out the garbage like everyone should.

Then he shook off the dust and held his head high
and headed back home to his perch in the sky
where he had acorns to eat and fur to keep warm
and branches to keep off the rain in a storm.

With all he had lost and as far as he'd drifted,
something was returning; a weight had been lifted.
And pricking his ears, he heard a faint tune
from a tree pointing up through the sky at the moon.

Climbing, he thought he might know what it *could* be.
Sitting, he knew he was right where he *should* be.

Then opening his ears, recognizing the song,
Rahoola Raccoon started humming along.